My First Ramadan

Karen Katz

SQUARE
FISH

Henry Holt and Company • New York

Look! There is the new moon in the sky.

Now we will begin our holiday called Ramadan (RAH-mah-dahn), a holy month for Muslims all around the world.

For one month Muslims will fast from sunup to sundown.

That means they will not eat or drink anything all day long.

This year I am bigger, and I will try to fast for the first time.

Daddy and I read about Ramadan in the Koran (kur-AHN), our holy book.

We fast because it helps us to concentrate on our faith.

It also reminds us to be thankful for all we have.

In the morning before the sun comes up, Mama makes a big breakfast.

We call it suhoor (suh-HOOR).

We share buttery eggs, toast, fluffy pancakes, fresh berries, and orange juice.

I eat and eat until I am so full!

Daddy leads us in a morning prayer
called fajr (FAH-jar). We pray five
times every day.

Muslims follow a religion called
Islam.

That means "peace" in Arabic.

I go off to school for the day.

It will be hard not to eat or drink.

We stay busy at school making
calendars for Ramadan.

Sometimes we learn songs and
play games.

At the end of the day, as the sun begins to set, we get ready for our evening meal.

Before we sit down to eat, we wash our hands and eat a sweet date, just like Muslims did almost 1,400 years ago.

That is when the prophet Muhammad first taught his followers to break their fast with a date and a sip of water.

At last it is time for iftar (if-TAHR), our evening meal.

We eat on the floor to keep our special tradition.
We say a prayer, called Maghrib (MAH-grib),
and then it's time to eat!

I am so hungry. Everything tastes so good!

We go to the mosque to pray.

The mosque looks beautiful standing

tall against the starry night.

It is like magic.

After four weeks have passed,
I look up at the sky to see if there
is a sliver of the new moon again.
Yes! We all see it!
This means that Ramadan will
end tomorrow.

We gather the next day in the town square to celebrate Eid al-Fitr (EED al-FITR), the end of Ramadan.

I see Muslims from Asia, Europe, Africa, Australia, North America, and South America.

I go with Daddy to say the Eid prayer.
We feel happy to be together.
Mama and my sister pray together in
a different room.

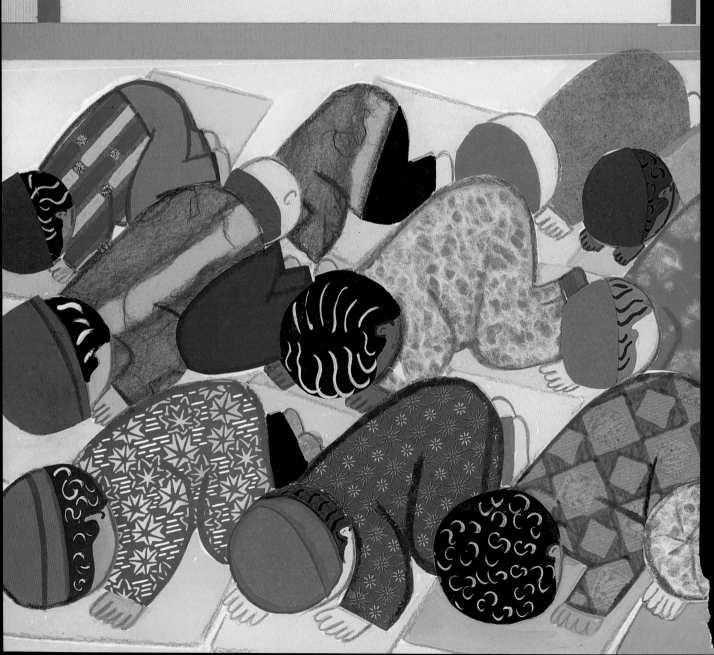

When the prayer has ended, we say,
"Eid mubarak!" (EED mu-BAHR-ak),
which means "Have a happy and
blessed Eid!"

At last we have a party with presents and games!

All my relatives are there.

We are happy that we have celebrated another Ramadan together.

To all the kids around the world who celebrate
in many different and wonderful ways.

Thanks to Kate and Laurent.

A Note About Ramadan

Ramadan is the most sacred time of the year for more
than one billion Muslims all over the world. It is the
ninth month of the Islamic calendar, and it begins with
the appearance of the new moon. Muslims believe that,
during this month in AD 610, Allah revealed the words
of the Koran to Muhammad. Ramadan is a time to
pray, fast, and help those in need—all important parts
of Muslim life. When Ramadan ends, at the sighting of
the next month's new moon, there is a three-day festival
called Eid al-Fitr. Ramadan is a time of togetherness for
Muslim families and friends.

SQUARE FISH

An Imprint of Macmillan
175 Fifth Avenue, New York, NY 10010
mackids.com

Square Fish books may be purchased for business or promotional use.
For information on bulk purchases, please contact the Macmillan Corporate and Premium Sales
Department at (800) 221-7945 x5442 or by e-mail at specialmarkets@macmillan.com.

Library of Congress Cataloging-in-Publication Data
Katz, Karen.
My first Ramadan / Karen Katz.—1st ed.
p.   cm.
Summary: A boy observes the Muslim holy month of Ramadan with his family.

ISBN 978-1-250-06268-0 (paperback)

Originally published in the United States by Henry Holt and Company, LLC
First Square Fish Edition: 2015
Book designed by Laurent Linn
Square Fish logo designed by Filomena Tuosto

10   9   8   7   6

AR: 2.8 / LEXILE: AD700L

The artist used collage and mixed media to create the illustrations for this book.